THE TEAM

WITHDRAWN

THE TEAM

David Bedford

Illustrated by Keith Brumpton

LITTLE HARE

www.littleharebooks.com

For Ali Lavau
—DB

Little Hare Books
8/21 Mary Street, Surry Hills
NSW 2010 AUSTRALIA

www.littleharebooks.com

The Football Machine *first published 2003*
Top of the League *first published 2003*
Soccer Camp *first published 2004*

This edition published 2007

National Library of Australia
Cataloguing-in-Publication entry

Bedford, David, 1969- .
The team.

For children.
ISBN 978 1 921272 04 2

1. Soccer - Juvenile fiction. I. Title.

823.92

Cover design by Serious Business
Set in 13.5/21 Giovanni by Asset Typesetting Pty Ltd
Printed in China by Imago

5 4 3 2 1

Contents

Prof Gertie   Darren   Harvey   Rita   Matt   Steffi   Mark 1

THE FOOTBALL MACHINE

Chapter 1

Eight–nil!

How could The Team lose eight–nil?

"We're rubbish," muttered Harvey. "Rubbish, rubbish, rubbish!"

The Team sat in the centre circle after the match. They were covered in mud, and too tired to move.

"We're not *that* bad," said Rita, as she picked dried freckles of mud from her face.

Harvey got slowly to his feet. "We are that bad," he said. "And we're getting worse."

Harvey walked home in his socks, dragging his boots behind him. Football was the only thing Harvey was good at — and he was still rubbish.

When Harvey reached Baker Street, there was a noise like thunder.

"Haaarrveyyy!"

It sounded like an aeroplane was landing on his head. Harvey ducked. Then he looked up.

Baker Street was on a hill. At the top of the hill was Harvey's house. Next door to Harvey's house there was a tall tower shaped like a rocket, with a window at the top.

Professor Gertie, Harvey's neighbour, was leaning from the window. She was wearing a bright yellow mask with a long beak, like a duck with its mouth open.

"It's me!" boomed Professor Gertie's voice. "I'm wearing my Shouting Mask! I've just invented it! Did you win?"

"No!" shouted Harvey.

"Oh, rats! Come up!"

Harvey walked slowly up the hill to the tower. He ducked inside the round door and climbed the twisting stairs. Professor Gertie was waiting for him at the top. She pulled off her Shouting Mask.

"What score?" Professor Gertie asked.

"Eight–nil," said Harvey.

"Double rats!" said Professor Gertie. "The Team aren't very good, are they?"

"We're rubbish," Harvey agreed.

"What about the Bouncing Boots?" Professor Gertie had glued springs to the bottom of Harvey's football boots. "Did they help you jump?"

"Yeah," said Harvey. "But I couldn't *stop* jumping. I knocked over Steffi, Matt and Paolo. Then I bounced on Darren, on Rita, in the sandpit, and landed on the referee. The ref made me take my boots off and play in my socks. And he gave me a yellow card."

"What about the Smoke Machine?" Professor Gertie had sewn a miniature Smoke Machine into Harvey's shorts.

Harvey turned around. There was a large hole in the back of his shorts, with burn marks around the edge. Through the hole you could see Harvey's shiny red underpants.

"The Fireproof Underpants worked!" said Professor Gertie proudly.

"Yeah," said Harvey. "They got a bit hot, though."

"Was there lots of smoke?"

"Lots," said Harvey. "I got the ball, turned on the Smoke Machine, and — whoosh! — no one could see where I was. I nearly scored! But there was so much smoke that I couldn't see the goal. Then nobody could see anything at all. The ref said I had to stop making smoke or he'd send me off."

"Stupid ref!" said Professor Gertie.

"He doesn't like me," said Harvey. "Not since I bounced on him."

"Next week we'll show him!" cried Professor Gertie. "I'm going to invent something so brilliant that you won't be able to lose."

"I'm not wearing Fireproof Underpants again," said Harvey. "They itch."

"I've got a better idea!" said Professor Gertie. She took her pencil from behind her ear and opened her notebook. "Tell me how you play football."

Harvey thought for a minute. "We chase the ball," he said. "And we tackle to get the ball. Then we try to *keep* the ball …"

"What else?" said Professor Gertie, writing a list.

Harvey scratched his head. There *was* something else. What was it? Oh yeah. "We're *supposed* to score goals," Harvey said. "But we haven't done that yet."

"Tut tut!" Professor Gertie stuck her pencil in her mouth and read out her list.

"How To Play Football
Chase
Tackle
Keep the ball
Score goals.

Now, which of these do you do badly?"

"All of them," said Harvey.

Later that night, Harvey was woken by bang-clatter-blop noises coming from Professor Gertie's tower.

Suddenly, there was a flash of lightning. Then a voice Harvey had never heard before said, "Aw, shucks!", and a strange rubbery smell drifted in through his bedroom window…

Professor Gertie was making something. What could it be? And would it really be good enough to help The Team win at last?

Chapter 2

Harvey didn't see Professor Gertie all that week. She had locked herself in her tower and wouldn't answer the door. But on Saturday morning, when Harvey left his house to go to the game, he found Professor Gertie waiting for him.

There was something waiting with her. Something strange. Something *very* strange.

It was wearing a white football shirt with a large red star on it — just like Harvey. But its head looked like it was made from an old rubbish bin covered in pink jelly. Its nose was a plug. And its eyes were red lights, like the scanners at a supermarket checkout. Harvey thought he saw one of the eyes wink at him.

"Er ... hello," Harvey said.

"He won't answer back," said Professor Gertie.

"Can't he talk?" said Harvey.

"No," said Professor Gertie. "His brain is pure football. He chases. He tackles. He keeps the ball. *And* he scores goals. He's a Football Machine, and he's programmed to win! Watch."

Professor Gertie pressed the red star on the Football Machine's shirt. The Football Machine started stretching and jumping up and down.

"He's a bit creaky," said Harvey.

Professor Gertie took an oilcan from the pocket of her lab coat and oiled the Football Machine's joints.

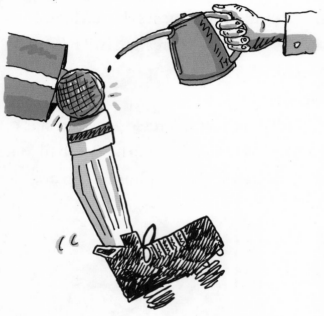

"His body is metal," she explained, "and he's covered from head to foot with Squidgy Skin. Bouncing Boots are built in and he has a top speed of sixty kilometres an hour. These are Skidders, for braking. And this is a Spinner, for turning."

As the Football Machine demonstrated the Spinner, Harvey asked, "What's his name?"

"I call him Football Machine Mark 1," said Professor Gertie. "Mark 1 means that he's the first of his kind — number one."

"I'll call him Mark 1," Harvey decided.

"Good!" said Professor Gertie. "Now remember, press his button once for warm-up exercises, twice for play, and three times to turn him off."

"How do I get him to follow me to the field?"

"That's easy," said Professor Gertie. "Just hold his hand."

"No way!"

"Go on!" Professor Gertie put one of Mark 1's hands into Harvey's. It felt squidgy — and warm. "Now off you go!"

Harvey led Mark 1 to the bottom of the hill, and turned the corner out of Baker Street. When he was sure Professor Gertie couldn't see him anymore, Harvey tried to pull his hand away, but Mark 1 wouldn't let go. Harvey pulled harder, but Mark 1's grip was as strong as steel.

"I give up!" said Harvey, and Mark 1's eyes blinked.

When they got to the football field, everyone stared.

"Harvey?" said Darren. "What are you *doing*?"

Harvey blushed. "This is Mark 1. He's a Football Machine and he's going to help us win," he explained.

"Why are you holding his hand?" asked Rita.

"To make him follow," said Harvey.

The Team were not impressed.

Then the Ham Football Furies arrived. They were dressed in yellow and black, and looked like a swarm of wasps. Their captain started laughing.

"Is that your star player?" he said. "Do you have to hold his hand in case he falls over?" All the Ham players laughed.

"It's embarrassing!" whispered Darren. "Harvey's machine can't play."

"Yes he can!" said Rita angrily. "We're one short anyway, because Steffi's on holiday. And it will teach the Furies a lesson if Mark 1 helps us win."

"He'll probably just get in our way," muttered Darren.

Rita said, "If he's no good, we'll take him off. Okay, Harvey?"

"Yeah," said Harvey.

The Team got into position. Ham were still laughing as they kicked off.

Harvey pressed Mark 1's button twice for "play", then let go of his hand.

"Aw, shucks!" said Mark 1.

"He can talk!" said Rita.

"He's not supposed to," said Harvey. He thought he saw a funny look in Mark 1's eyes. Then Harvey had to chase Ham to get the ball, and he was too busy to see if Mark 1 really could play football or not.

At last Harvey got the ball.

"Pass, Harvey!" his team mates called.

But Harvey couldn't see anyone to pass to, and a Ham forward took the ball off him. The Ham players cheered.

Then — *whoooom!* — something shot past Harvey so fast the wind blew his hair across his eyes. He could just make out a white shirt with a red star on it, and a pink-jelly head shaped like a rubbish bin.

Chapter 3

Harvey stood still and watched in amazement.

Mark 1 pounced on the ball. He dodged left. He dodged right. Then he ran straight towards the Ham goal. Four Ham defenders closed in. Harvey waited for the crunching tackle but — *zzooomm!* — Mark 1 shot forward like a rocket. The Ham goalie watched him nervously. *Skid — swivel — shoot —*

"GOAL!"

Darren and Rita jumped into Harvey's arms, and they all fell over, laughing. So did the rest of The Team.

"He's brilliant!" said Rita.

Ham kicked off. Mark 1 swooped in and took the ball. Every Ham player raced after him. But they couldn't catch him. Mark 1 swerved in and — *shoot* —

Goal!

Ham kicked off again. They tried to hide the ball from Mark 1 by making a circle around it. *Boing!* Mark 1 jumped inside the circle, trapped the ball between his ankles, and jumped out again. *Boing!*

The Ham goalie pulled Mark 1's shirt, but
it didn't slow Mark 1 down. He ran the ball
straight into the net.

Goal!

Goal! Goal! Goal!

At half-time, The Team were dancing and
cheering.

"Twenty-seven–nil!" shouted Rita. "I don't believe it!"

"He's beating them single-handed!" said Darren.

But the Ham captain was shouting at the ref. "It's not fair! He's not real!"

"You weren't complaining when you first saw him!" said Rita furiously.

The ref looked Mark 1 up and down. He looked at Mark 1's Bouncing Boots, and frowned. "What's your name, son?"

Mark 1's eyes flashed.

"He's a machine!" said the Ham captain. "That's why his head's like a rubbish bin. Harvey made him!"

"Aw, shucks!" said Mark 1. "Harveee diddle make meee!"

"What's he on about?" the ref asked Harvey. "Is he a machine?"

"Sort of," said Harvey.

The ref blew his whistle. "Game void! You can play again next week. And *you*," he said, pointing at Harvey, "if I catch you breaking the rules again, I'll send you off for the rest of the season!"

The Team groaned.

"The ref's got it in for you," said Darren. "Ever since you bounced on him."

"I suppose it *was* cheating," said Harvey.

"Next week," said Rita, "we'll beat them fair and square."

"We're the worst team in the league," Harvey reminded her. "Next week, Ham will slaughter us."

Harvey took Mark 1's hand and led him home. Mark 1's smile seemed to have drooped. "Sorreee Harveee," he said sadly.

"It wasn't your fault," said Harvey. Then he remembered. "Hey! You *can* talk, can't you? Go on, say something else. Say 'The Team are rubbish.'"

But Mark 1 said nothing. The lights in his eyes had gone out.

Chapter 4

"What happened?"

Professor Gertie was leaning from her window, wearing her Shouting Mask. Harvey was too depressed to answer, and he let Mark 1 carry him up the twisting stairs.

Professor Gertie was bouncing up and down at the top. "You won!" she said. "I know you did. **THE TEAM! THE TEAM! WELL DONE THE TEAM!**"

"We *did* win …" Harvey began slowly, "until half-time, anyway. Then Ham complained."

"What about?"

"Mark 1. The ref said he's against the rules. We have to play the game again next week."

"Rot the ref!" said Professor Gertie. "He'll have to change the rules."

"He won't do that," said Harvey.

Professor Gertie sniffed. "Was he good, then?" she asked, watching as Mark 1 played keep-ups with a rolled-up sock.

"Brilliant," said Harvey. "Best player I've ever seen. Everyone on our team loved him."

"Oh dear," said Professor Gertie. "That makes it a double waste to feed him to Masher."

"Who?"

"Masher. He chews up old inventions."

Professor Gertie went to her inventing table and lifted up the tablecloth. Underneath there was a monstrous machine like a giant crab. It had black eyes, a large grinning mouth, grinding teeth and a long, grabbing arm. Harvey imagined it chewing up Mark 1. It was horrible.

"You can't feed Mark 1 to Masher!" said Harvey. "You just can't!"

"I never like mashing my inventions," said Professor Gertie. "But don't forget, Mark 1 is only a machine."

"He's not! He's learned to talk. Go on, Mark 1, say something!"

Mark 1 was busy jumping up to head the lampshade.

"I have to mash him," said Professor Gertie. "I haven't got room to keep inventions that don't work."

"He does work!" said Harvey.

"But the ref won't let him play," said Professor Gertie. "So he's useless."

Mark 1 came over and lifted Harvey into the air. "Stop it!" said Harvey irritably.

"He's showing you how to head the lampshade," said Professor Gertie.

That gave Harvey an idea.

"I know!" he said. "Mark 1 can be our trainer. We can practise against him. So he's *not* useless and he doesn't have to be mashed!"

"Good idea!" said Professor Gertie, suddenly excited again. "And next week you'll need new Bouncing Boots, too. And you could try the Smoke Machine again ..."

"We can't," said Harvey. "The ref said no inventions."

"I don't like that ref! What about Tackle Arms attached to your ankles?"

"No," said Harvey. "The only thing we need is someone to cheer us on. Nobody ever does that."

"I could do it!" Professor Gertie opened her notebook, and started scribbling a new list. "I'll need a scarf…" she muttered. "And a hat … This time, I'm really going to help The Team win!"

That week, The Team trained every day. They learned how to get the ball from Mark 1, *and* how to keep it from him.

Darren said, "No one's going to score past me! Watch!"

He threw the ball to Mark 1, and Mark 1 shot at the goal. Darren dived full stretch and saved it.

"Great!" The Team cheered.

"Aw, shucks!" said Mark 1. He ran to fetch the ball and try again.

"All you have to do is score a goal, Harvey," said Rita. "Then we'll win!"

"Why don't *you* score?" said Harvey.

"I can't," said Rita, shaking her head. "When I get near the goal my legs turn to jelly. You're our best player, Harvey. *You* have to score!"

That was the real problem, thought Harvey. He had never scored, except in practice. So what chance did he have of scoring against the Ham Football Furies? It wasn't Mark 1 who was useless. It was Harvey.

Chapter 5

On Friday, the night before the match, Harvey had a terrible dream.

He dreamed that Masher came looking for him at school, and then chased him home, biting at his ankles. Masher wanted to chew Harvey up, because Harvey was useless.

Harvey ran and ran — then woke up. The sun was shining and it was just an ordinary Saturday morning ...

Harvey looked at the clock. The match! He'd be late!

He pulled on his football kit and ran all the way to the field.

The Ham Furies were already there. When their captain saw Harvey, he shouted, "Where's Rubbish Bin Head? Wouldn't he let you hold his hand?" The Ham players exploded with laughter.

The Team huddled close in a circle, so no one could hear them whispering. "You were nearly late!" said Rita. "Where's Mark 1?"

"He should be here," said Harvey, out of breath. "Professor Gertie's coming, too. She's going to cheer us on." He looked around the field. Where *was* Professor Gertie? She'd never let him down before. Ever.

Suddenly, there was a roar of laughter.

"I think she's arrived," said Rita.

Harvey turned to look. "Oh, no!"

Professor Gertie was dressed as a glittering red star. She bounced up and down on Bouncing Sandals. She blew Finger Whistles. She rattled Ankle Bells. And she waved a Clattering Scarf.

The Ham players rolled on the ground, crying with laughter. "Not another *star* player?" their captain said. "This one's a real super-*star*!"

"Sorry we're late!" Professor Gertie called to Harvey. "It took me ages to get Mark 1 to wear his hat!"

"I'm not surprised," whispered Darren.

Mark 1 was trying to hide behind Professor Gertie. He was wearing a frilly red hat with glittery letters spelling The Team, and his pink-jelly face had turned red with embarrassment.

The ref blew his whistle. Harvey kicked off — straight to a Ham player.

"You're a joke, Harvey!" said the Ham captain. But suddenly the Ham team were quiet, holding their ears.

"The Team! The Team! Come on The Team!"

It was like thunder and an earthquake rolled together.

"What's that?" yelled Darren.

"Professor Gertie's Shouting Mask!" called Harvey.

"It's like having ten thousand fans cheering for us!" said Rita. "She's brilliant!"

"Yeah," said Harvey. "She is." Professor Gertie didn't always get things right, but she *never* let anyone down.

The Team got the ball and attacked the Ham goal.

"The Team! The Team! Come on The Team!"

The Team were good. Their training had worked, and Ham couldn't get the ball.

Not until Harvey gave it to them.

"Aw, shucks, Harveee!" shouted Mark 1.

Now Ham were attacking. They weren't laughing anymore. They headed straight for Darren's goal.

Suddenly the ball was flying into the top corner and it was —

"Saved!"

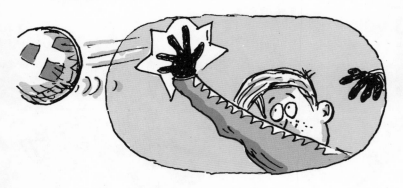

"Told you!" said Darren. "No one scores past me!"

But Ham were now playing better than they ever had, and Darren had to save shot after shot.

After half-time it was worse. The Team were tired, and they had to defend all the time.

"**One minute to go!**" called Professor Gertie, who was biting her Finger Whistles nervously.

Darren threw the ball to Harvey. Harvey passed it to Rita, but she passed it straight back. None of The Team wanted the ball, and Harvey didn't know what to do. He needed help. Bouncing Boots or a Smoke Machine or Ankle Tacklers or ...

"Doo itt, Harveeee!"

It was Mark 1, wearing Professor Gertie's Shouting Mask. How come Mark 1 could talk? Nobody had shown him how. He just...did it.

Suddenly, Harvey darted away, dodging past two Ham players. That was it! Harvey didn't need Bouncing Boots or *anything*! He just had to DOO ITT.

"Go on, Harveee!"

Harvey zoomed past the ref, who already had his whistle in his mouth. The game was almost over!

Harvey put on a burst of speed. Whooom! The goal was straight ahead and he was running out of time! Skid. Swivel. *Shoot —*

The ball seemed to move in slow motion, like a balloon. The Ham goalie jumped and tried to grab it out of the air, but he missed. Harvey's shot floated gently into the top corner of the net.

"Goooooaaaalllll!!!"

The ref blew his whistle to end the game. The Team had won!

Mark 1 raced over to Harvey, lifted him onto his shoulders and bounced him around the field.

"M-make him s-stop!" called Harvey. "I'm g-gonna b-be s-sick!"

"I can't stop him!" yelled Professor Gertie. "He's re-programmed himself. He pressed his own button *four* times. It makes him celebrate!"

Ham's captain ran over to complain. "No celebrations allowed!" he whined. "It was a lucky goal, that's all."

"That's right!" said the ref, who was angry because he hadn't blown his whistle before Harvey scored. "I'm turning this machine OFF!" He caught Mark 1 and started pressing his button.

"You shouldn't have done that!" said Professor Gertie.

"Why not?" said the ref.

"Because you pressed his button five times. And five times means ..."

Before she could finish, Mark 1 dropped Harvey, lifted up the ref and the Ham captain, and ran away with them so no one could turn him off.

"What does five times do?" Harvey asked Professor Gertie.

"Mark 1's taught himself how to *juggle*!" giggled Professor Gertie. "But don't worry! He'll bring them back when his battery runs down."

"Now we *can* celebrate!" said Harvey. "The Team! The Team! We are The Team!"

And The Team celebrated winning for the first, and best, time ever.

TOP OF THE LEAGUE

Chapter 1

Harvey raced back to The Team's goal to defend, scrunching his shoulders against the rain, which was like a waterfall drumming on his head.

He saw Darren, The Team's goalie, wipe his eyes, leaving long streaks of mud across his face. The rain had turned the goal area into a swamp, and Darren's feet had sunk up to his ankles as he crouched, ready to dive.

The Rovers striker outpaced Matt and Steffi and the rest of The Team's defence. Harvey put on a last burst of speed, but he was too late. The striker flicked a shot over Darren's head.

Darren jumped. At least, he tried to. But the sticky mud held his feet as if they were stuck in concrete. Darren fell over backwards and The Team watched the ball sail towards the goal.

Harvey groaned. It was nil–nil, with only five minutes to go, and Darren had just missed a shot he should have caught easily.

Luckily, the ball hit the crossbar — DONK!

— and rebounded away for a corner. "Phew!" Darren sighed in relief as he pulled his feet out of the mud. Matt and Steffi were furious, though.

"You mudbrain!" shouted Steffi. "They nearly scored!"

"You didn't even dive!" screamed Matt. "This is the biggest game we've ever played, remember?"

The Team had been getting better all season, climbing slowly towards the top of the league. They needed just one more point to be sure of winning the league trophy — and a trip to Soccer Camp.

"You try goalkeeping in a bog!" Darren yelled back at Matt and Steffi.

"Try keeping your eyes open, boggy man!" said Steffi.

Before Darren could reply, the ball was kicked high from the corner. Darren launched himself into the air to catch it. Steffi, Matt and two Rovers forwards jumped to head it. They all missed the ball, and Rita booted it up the field for Harvey to chase.

"Wait!" shouted Rita, and everyone stopped. "Where's Darren?"

Harvey put his foot on the ball and looked around. There was no one in goal.

"He was there when the ball came over," said Rita. "Then he just … disappeared!"

SLUUUUURCH!

A shape rose up from the swamp. Brown water and lumps of mud ran down its arms and fell from the fingers of its goalkeeper's gloves. The thing slowly opened its eyes.

"Darren!" said Rita. "Are you all right?"

Darren nodded, and a lump of mud the size of an orange rolled off his head and landed at his feet with a plop.

"I told you to keep your eyes open!" scolded Steffi.

"Great dive!" snorted Matt. "But you should take your boots off before you go swimming!"

As the rain washed the mud from Darren's face, Harvey saw that there were angry purple splotches on his cheeks.

"Two minutes to go!" the ref called.

Harvey suddenly remembered the ball at his feet. The Rovers midfielders, who had stopped to stare at Darren, were closing in on him. He spun away from them and sprinted towards the Rovers' goal. He swerved past one defender, then another. But the third one tackled him, and the Rovers were back on the attack.

Harvey was running back to defend when he saw it happen.

Darren was still arguing with Steffi and Matt.

The rest of The Team were watching the argument.

"Look out!" cried Harvey.

It was too late. The Rovers striker shot, and Darren didn't even see the ball as it flew past his knee and into the net for a goal.

The ref blew the final whistle. For the first time in months, The Team had lost.

"Oh, you're USELESS!" Steffi shouted at Darren.

"WORSE than useless!" yelled Matt.

Darren pushed past them without speaking, and stormed off across the field.

"Darren!" called Harvey. "Don't go! It wasn't your fault!"

"Of course it was his fault," said Matt. "He's supposed to be our ace goalie, and he couldn't even catch a cold."

Darren turned to yell, "I don't care! I've had ENOUGH!"

It looked like the purple splotches on Darren's cheeks had spread over the whole of his face.

"We're better off without him," said Steffi. "Anyway, we've still got one more game, and one more chance to win. We'll just find someone else to go in goal. No one could be worse than Darren."

"We don't need anyone else in goal," said Harvey angrily. "Darren is The Team's goalie. He's saved us loads of times, so give him a break!"

"I'll talk to Darren," said Rita. "I'm sure he'll come back."

But Harvey wasn't so sure. He'd never seen anyone get so upset they grew purple splotches on their face. Harvey didn't think Darren would come back — ever.

Chapter 2

Harvey trudged home through the puddles.
Waves of water gushed from his soggy football
boots, but he hardly noticed.

He was worried about The Team. They used
to be the worst in the league. Then Harvey's
neighbour, Professor Gertie, had invented
Mark 1, the Football Machine.

With the robot's help in training, The Team were now on their way to being the best.

At first, winning had been the most fun Harvey and The Team had ever had.

Then things had started to change. The closer they got to the top of the league, the more they argued.

Harvey was worried about something else, too. Mark 1 and Professor Gertie should have been at the game to cheer The Team on. What could have happened to them?

Harvey turned into Baker Street, squelched up the hill to the top, and stopped at Professor Gertie's inventing tower.

The tower rose tall and straight into the grey sky, like a rocket about to take off. Harvey knocked on the door.

He heard shouting, then feet stamping on metal stairs. Finally, the door was yanked open and Professor Gertie stood there, red-faced and glowering.

"Oh, hello Harvey," she said, trying not to sound as angry she looked. "How are you today?"

"You missed the game," said Harvey. "And we lost."

Normally, Professor Gertie would have wanted to know all about the game, but now she simply shook her head. "I lost track of time," she muttered. "I'm sorry, Harvey. Come up."

Harvey followed her up the twisting stairs into the tower. "Who was shouting?" he asked.

Professor Gertie frowned. "That was me," she admitted. "Mark 1 has stopped doing what he's told. He keeps arguing."

"Just like The Team," said Harvey, and he explained about Darren storming off.

"If I could invent a cure for arguing, I'd be rich," said Professor Gertie gloomily. "The problem is, there's no quick fix."

Harvey was disappointed. Inventors were always coming up with quick fixes. He thought that's what inventors were for.

Harvey found Mark 1 in the living room. The robot was the perfect football machine. He had a top speed of sixty kilometres an hour, a Spinner for turning, Skidders for braking, and Bouncing Boots for jumping. The brain inside his rubbish-bin head was dedicated purely to football.

At the moment, Mark 1 was lying on the sofa, watching cartoons.

"Hey," said Harvey.

"Ho," said Mark 1, giving Harvey a friendly flash of his red laser eyes before turning back to the television.

"I don't know what's wrong with him," whispered Professor Gertie. "When he's not out training The Team, he sulks in his room or watches television. He won't listen to anything I say."

"Maybe his ears aren't working?"

"I checked," said Professor Gertie. "His Listeners are fine. He's *pretending* not to hear. Watch."

She picked up her Shouting Mask from the top of the television, and strapped it onto her face. The Shouting Mask was another of Professor Gertie's inventions. It amplified her voice so she sounded like a thousand people shouting at once. Now she'd found a new use for it. She bellowed,

"Mark 1! Take your feet off the sofa!"

"Mark 1! Tidy your room!"

"Mark 1! Why don't you answer me WHEN I'M TALKING TO YOU?!!!"

Harvey had to cover his ears with his hands. He could easily guess why Mark 1 was pretending not to hear.

"Don't you think," he said to Professor Gertie carefully, "that you might be, just a little bit, nagging him?"

Professor Gertie, who was still wearing the Shouting Mask, looked like a giant, angry duck. **"Me? Nagging? Of course not! All I'm asking is for Mark 1 to be a bit tidier and DO**

AS I SAY! It's all right for him — going out and training The Team and enjoying himself. I'm the one who has to stay at home washing his socks and tidying up and doing so many other things that I don't even have time for my inventions!"

Mark 1 flashed his eyes at Harvey again, then tied one of his socks over his earholes and started bouncing his boots up and down on the sofa.

Professor Gertie carried on nagging Mark 1 through her Shouting Mask.

Harvey, with his hands still covering his ears, left them to it. If Professor Gertie wasn't going to help, he would have to fix The Team's problems himself.

As he left the tower he saw Rita running up the hill.

"I talked to Darren," she called out. "He's not angry now!"

"That's great!" said Harvey. But Rita didn't look happy.

"Actually, it's not great," she said. "Because he still doesn't want to come back. He said playing on The Team gives him purple splotches, and it isn't fun anymore."

Harvey sighed. "The Team is the problem," he said. "Not Darren. We've got to stop The

Team from arguing. But Professor Gertie said there are no quick fixes."

"So what are we going to do next Saturday?" said Rita. "It's our last match, and it's against the Diamonds."

"The best team in the league," said Harvey gloomily.

"Except for the Team," said Rita. "And we still only need one point to win the trophy."

Harvey sighed. "Without a goalie we won't have a chance."

Rita reached into her back pocket and brought out two soggy goalkeeper's gloves.

"Darren gave me these. I'm willing to go in goal if I have to."

Harvey brightened. "Are you any good?"

"No," said Rita. "I'm rubbish."

Chapter 3

"You're not that bad," said Harvey.

Rita and Harvey had practised every night since Saturday. Now it was Thursday, and the rest of The Team would be turning up soon for their training session with Mark 1. For the first time in a week, it had stopped raining.

"Try this." Harvey drifted the ball towards goal. Rita jumped to catch it, but the ball slipped through her hands.

"Told you," she said. "I'm rubbish."

Harvey tried an even slower shot, rolling the ball along the ground. Rita bent down and gathered it up, but the ball knocked hard against her chin and Harvey heard her teeth rattle.

"You okay?" said Harvey.

"I jutht bit my tongue," said Rita, with a grimace. "Have another thot."

"My turn!" Steffi raced onto the field, intercepted the ball and kicked it easily into the goal.

"You've got to watch what's going on," Steffi said. "That was Darren's problem, too."

"Don't tell me what to do," said Rita, marching out of the goal towards Steffi.

Suddenly there was a shout. "Yoo-hooo!" They all turned to see Professor Gertie hurrying across the field with Mark 1, who was carrying a box.

As they drew near, the box slipped from Mark 1's hands.

"Did you see that?" Rita whispered. "Mark 1 dropped it on purpose."

"They're not getting along," replied Harvey.

Professor Gertie looked at Mark 1 crossly, then picked up two of her inventions. "You didn't think I'd let you down, did you?" she said, turning to Rita. "I put the housework on hold, and directed all my efforts into these. Mark 1 helped, by doing what he was TOLD for a change!"

Harvey and Rita examined the inventions. They looked to Harvey like the kind of gloves King Arthur and his knights wore, except that each finger ended in a suction cup.

"They're Anti-Goal Gauntlets!" said Professor Gertie, beaming.

As the rest of The Team arrived, Rita pulled off her old goalkeeper's gloves and Professor Gertie pushed the gauntlets on.

"They're heavy," Rita said.

"I had to use armour-plated steel," Professor Gertie explained. "So the Finger Rockets don't burn through."

"Finger Rockets?" said Rita nervously.

"They shoot out when you stretch your fingers wide. Try it!"

Rita stood in goal, holding the heavy gloves as far away from her body as she could. She didn't like the sound of Finger Rockets.

"Ready, steady, go!" said Professor Gertie excitedly.

"Let me shoot," said Steffi with a mischievous grin. She took a long run up, and fired the ball shouting "Goal!" as soon as the ball had left her foot.

Rita reached for the ball, stretching her fingers wide.

The Anti-Goal Gauntlets started to vibrate and grow hot. Then there were eight tiny puffs of smoke, and eight tiny screams as the gloves' fingertips shot out like fireworks.

Three of them hit the ball, and stuck.

The fingertips were still attached to Rita's gloves by elastic bands. She yanked her wrists and the ball sprang easily towards her. She caught it between both hands and called, "Saved!"

Everyone except Steffi cheered.

Professor Gertie peeled the suction cups from the ball. "Now clap your hands," she said. "The elastic bands will wind back in so the Finger Rockets are ready to fire again."

Rita clapped. Nothing happened.

She clapped harder. Still nothing happened.

Professor Gertie stared dangerously at Mark 1. "Did you put the Winders in like I told you to?"

Mark 1 pretended not to hear.

Professor Gertie's eyes nearly popped out of her head. She drew in a huge breath, but before she could shout Harvey said hastily, "What about your other inventions?"

Professor Gertie let her breath out in a long sigh. "Well, okay," she said, giving Mark 1 a final glare. "But the Finger Rockets were my favourite."

She picked up another pair of gloves from the ground.

Rita took off the Anti-Goal Gauntlets, and put the new gloves on. They didn't seem unusual at all, except for a coil of wire like an aerial stitched around each finger, and a tiny satellite dish on the end of each thumb.

"Sit down," said Professor Gertie. Harvey watched curiously as she screwed something to the bottom of Rita's boots. Now the boots looked like rollerskates, but instead of wheels, each one had a red-and-white striped skirt.

"Are they ... *hovercrafts*?" asked Harvey.

"I call them Gliders," said Professor Gertie as she pulled Rita to her feet. "When Rita reaches for the ball, her thumbs will tell the Gliders which way to go. And the gloves have Sticky Palms — but don't worry about that now."

Harvey lined up the ball, and Rita clomped clumsily to the centre of the goal. The Gliders were so heavy she could barely lift her feet.

"Ready?" said Harvey. Rita nodded, and he stroked the ball high towards the net.

Rita reached out her hands. Suddenly, she started to glide. As she sailed quickly across the goal mouth, the ball hit her gloves — and stuck.

"The Sticky Palms work!" said Professor Gertie.

"Let's try it again!" said Rita. She went to throw Harvey the ball — but it stayed firmly stuck to her gloves.

Professor Gertie turned to Mark 1. "Did you mix some Anti-Sticky in with the Sticky so that the ball would come unstuck? I clearly remember telling you to!"

Mark 1 pretended not to hear, but Harvey saw a gleam of triumph flash across his laser eyes.

"Rats!" shouted Professor Gertie. "You've ruined all my inventions — and they worked, too!" Harvey thought she was going to explode like a Finger Rocket.

"They were brilliant," he said quickly. "But we couldn't have used them on Saturday. The ref doesn't allow inventions."

Professor Gertie pulled the sticky gloves off Rita and, with Rita and Harvey's help, tugged the ball free.

Harvey stood out of the way as she threw all her useless inventions back into their box. He had never seen her so grumpy before.

"Let's give Rita some more practice," Harvey said encouragingly.

"Good idea," said Matt. "She needs it!"

"She *really* needs it!" scoffed Steffi.

Rita put on Darren's ordinary goalkeeper's gloves and Mark 1 started firing shots at the goal. She didn't save even one.

"We're going to get hammered," groaned Steffi. "Rita's completely useless!"

Rita took off her gloves. "Find yourself another goalie, then," she said, and walked off across the field.

Matt turned to Steffi. "That's the second goalie you've scared away! Why don't you give everyone a break?"

"You started it!" said Steffi.

"You did, you mean!" said Matt.

Soon everyone was shouting.

Harvey watched Rita cross the field. She passed Professor Gertie and Mark 1, who were picking up the box Mark 1 had just dropped again. Professor Gertie was shouting as well.

"That's it!" Harvey bellowed. "The Team are FINISHED!"

But The Team were arguing so loudly that no one heard him.

Chapter 4

That night, Harvey had a dream. In it, he was Professor Harvey, and he lived in an inventing tower full of his own shiny, brilliant inventions.

It wasn't a pleasant dream, though. All day, people kept knocking on his door, begging him to fix their problems, and arguing with him when he said he didn't know how to.

"We used to like playing together," they said. "But now we hate it!"

"There's too much pressure! It's making us too nervous!"

They all had purple splotches on their faces.

Professor Harvey scratched his head, thinking. Suddenly, he had an idea. It was perfect! And so simple! Why hadn't he thought of it before?

Harvey woke up. His alarm clock was ringing and his bedroom was filled with bright sunlight. In his dream, Professor Harvey had just thought of a way to stop people arguing. If only Harvey could remember what it was.

He lay back on his bed and closed his eyes, trying to get back into the dream. But he couldn't.

He sat up again. Whenever Professor Gertie was trying to solve a problem, she wrote a list. Harvey grabbed one of his school notebooks and opened it at a fresh page.

He tried to imagine he really *was* Professor Harvey. He scratched his head like Professor Harvey did, and pretended his bedroom was Professor Harvey's inventing room. But he couldn't think of anything to write. Instead, he doodled a face in the corner of the page. He gave the face a shock of hair like Darren's. Then he drew splotches all over the face.

The Team were nervous because they wanted to win so badly. It was the nerves that were making them argue — and the arguing was making the nerves even worse.

Harvey put his pen to the top of the page and wrote, "How to Stop Arguing and Be a Team."

Then he wrote a list. Maybe if he showed it to Professor Gertie she could use it to invent something that stopped arguing.

Harvey had to knock three times on Professor Gertie's tower door before she opened it. She was holding a large yellow duster in each hand, and looked hot and busy.

Harvey told her about his list. But Professor Gertie didn't even look at the notebook Harvey was holding up. "You can't solve everything with a list, Harvey!" she snapped. "I should know that!"

Harvey heard banging from inside the tower. It sounded like an elephant jumping on a trampoline, and Harvey guessed that Mark 1 was bouncing up and down on the sofa. Professor Gertie roared and started back up the stairs into the tower. "Mark 1!" she hollered. "You are *supposed* to be cleaning your room!"

Harvey tore the list from his notebook and stuck it on a nail on Professor Gertie's door. There was nothing else he could do. Then he jogged down Baker Street to his school at the bottom of the hill.

Walking home from school that afternoon, Harvey heard a huge bang. He looked up the hill and saw a swirl of rainbow-coloured smoke rising from Professor Gertie's tower.

Harvey ran. When he reached the tower, there was already a crowd of people staring at it. The roof had completely blown off. Harvey looked about frantically.

In a shady spot by the side of the tower, two people were having a picnic.

"What happened?" Harvey asked breathlessly as he ran over. "Are you okay? What happened?"

"You've already asked that," said Professor Gertie, as Mark 1 poured her a cup of tea. Then she picked up an oilcan and oiled behind Mark 1's neck. Mark I shivered happily.

"One good turn deserves another," said Professor Gertie. "And all's well that ends well."

"Huh?" said Harvey, who was still wondering what was going on.

"We just had a silly, silly tiff," Professor Gertie explained. "I decided to clean Mark 1's room myself. So Mark 1 decided to clean my

Inventing Bench. Some chemicals got mixed together, and there was a small explosion."

"Boom!" said Mark 1 happily, clapping his hands together.

"It made us realise we *had* to stop arguing," said Professor Gertie. "Arguing is DANGEROUS. But we had no idea how to stop — until we found your clever list!"

She held up the page Harvey had torn from his notebook. "You've added two more ideas," said Harvey.

"Not me," said Professor Gertie. "Mark 1 wrote those. Well done, both of you!"

Harvey couldn't believe it. Had his list really made them stop arguing?

"We've decided to do everything as a team," said Professor Gertie. "That way, no one gets left out, and everything is fair." She took a piece of paper from her pocket, and Harvey saw that she and Mark 1 had made a list of their own. "Mark 1's going to have his own Inventing Bench next to mine," she said. "We'll each do half of the housework and washing. And from now on we'll *both* train The Team."

"If there is a Team," Harvey said miserably.

"But you know how to fix The Team's problems now, don't you?" said Professor Gertie. "Use your list!"

Harvey took the list from Professor Gertie, folded it up and put it in his pocket.

"It won't work," he said.

"Trry itt!" said Mark 1 as he buttered a scone and handed it to Professor Gertie.

Harvey still couldn't believe they were getting along so well. Maybe — just maybe — the list would work for The Team.

"Okay, I'll try it," he said, and for the first time all week, he managed a hopeful smile.

Chapter 5

On Saturday morning, Harvey awoke to the sound of rain hammering on his bedroom window. He groaned. Just the sort of weather to put everyone in a bad mood.

He splashed through puddles to the field, his soggy socks squelching, and all his hope evaporating. There was no way The Team would follow his stupid list. If he read it out, everyone would laugh, and then he might as well walk straight home again.

When he arrived at the field, he saw Rita warming up. "You're back!" he said. "What happened?"

"I didn't want to give in to Steffi and Matt," Rita said. "I'm a match for their insults any day — I'll just argue back!"

Harvey didn't like the sound of that. "Maybe you won't have to argue," he said.

While he waited for the rest of The Team to arrive, Harvey watched the Diamonds warming up. They looked organised and happy, like they knew they were going to win.

Harvey called The Team into a huddle. "I've got a plan," he said.

"Here we go," said Matt, pretending to yawn.

"This is our biggest game ever," Harvey continued. "If we want to win the league, *and* a trip to Soccer Camp, we either have to draw or win today."

"We already know that!" said Steffi scornfully.

"But if we keep arguing," Harvey went on, "we won't win anything. There won't even *be* a Team anymore. We've got to stop arguing!"

"Good plan," sniggered Matt. "I think that's *really* going to work, don't you, Steffi?"

Ignoring Matt, Harvey took a deep breath and read out his list.

"How to Stop Arguing and Be a Team
1. Ask, don't tell.
2. Discuss our problems.
3. Be positive and don't criticise."
Then he read out what Mark 1 had added:
"4. No nagging!
5. Bee happee!"

Matt took the list from him. "So this is your great plan?"

"Yeah," said Harvey.

Matt started to laugh. "Harvey, you're so funny!"

"Come on," said Steffi impatiently. "The ref's waiting. We haven't got time for Harvey's jokes."

The Team took their positions, with Matt still laughing loudly.

"Too bad, Harvey," said Rita as she headed for her goal. "Good try."

Harvey shrugged. He saw Professor Gertie and Mark 1 arrive together, chatting happily under a shared umbrella. At least the list had worked for them. But he still felt miserable. He was sure he was about to play his last-ever game with The Team.

Chapter 6

The Diamonds kicked off and Harvey chased after the ball, skidding and slipping in the mud. Finally, Steffi got the ball with a sliding tackle. She darted forward and was knocked over by a Diamonds defender. The ref awarded her a free kick in line with the Diamonds' goal.

"You take it," Steffi ordered Matt. "You're a better shot than me."

Matt looked furious. "How dare you tell me what to do!" he shouted. But as he turned his face away, Harvey saw him grin secretly.

Matt turned back to Steffi and declared, "Ask, don't tell!"

"Okay, okay!" said Steffi crossly. "Matt, would you please take this free kick?"

"Let's discuss it," said Matt, folding his arms. "That's what the list says to do, Steffi. I'm trying to help you here."

The Diamonds were laughing. So were most of The Team.

Steffi's face turned red. "Just take the free kick!" she yelled. "Why do you have to be so difficult all the time?"

Matt grinned and quoted from the list again. "Be positive and don't criticise."

Rita, who'd run up the field to see what the argument was about, tried to hide a smile behind her gloves. "And no nagging!" she reminded Steffi.

"Don't forget to bee happee!" finished Matt, who was laughing so hard he couldn't stand.

The rest of The Team were laughing too — all except Steffi, who was fuming, and Harvey, who was frowning thoughtfully. The Team were laughing instead of arguing. Had his list done that?

"That's enough!" said the ref. "The free kick can go to the Diamonds instead!"

The Diamonds took the kick quickly, and The Team ran back to defend. Rita reached her goal just in time. A Diamonds attacker was bearing down on her, drawing back his foot to shoot.

Steffi skidded into him, stopping the shot, but the ref's whistle screamed — the Diamonds had another free kick, this time right in front of Rita's goal.

While Harvey arranged a wall, Rita crouched low, keeping her eyes on the ball.

"That's good," said Darren. "But stand up more and think yourself big. It looks like he's going to blast it."

Rita turned her head. Darren was beside the goal. "You're back!" she said.

"Only to watch," said Darren.

"But your purple splotches have gone," said Rita. "You could play."

"Have The Team stopped arguing?" said Darren.

"We haven't argued for at least a minute," said Rita.

"Well that's a world record," said Darren grimly. Then he pointed, "Quick!"

Rita turned too late. The Diamond's defender had already blasted the ball straight at her, and it hit her square on the forehead.

Rita stumbled backwards and sat down in the mud.

The ball flew up in the air and came straight down again. This time it hit her on the top of the head and bounced backwards into the goal.

The Diamonds cheered.

"Rita!" yelled Steffi, standing over her as the rest of The Team ran up. Steffi's face had twisted in what Harvey thought was rage. But instead of shouting, Steffi started making a noise like a chicken clucking. At first, no one knew what she was doing.

"Is she laughing?" said Harvey at last.

"It's hard to tell," said Matt. "But I think so."

"I was wrong when I said Darren was useless!" Steffi spluttered. "Next to Rita, he's a genius!" She tried to pull Rita to her feet, still clucking madly.

"I'm glad you see the funny side," said Rita, smiling. "I know I'm hopeless and I wish we had a good goalie, but we don't."

"Yes we do," Steffi said, turning to Darren. "I'm sorry for what I said," she told him seriously. "But now we've got this crazy list that stops us arguing. It makes us laugh instead! So will you come back now, Darren? Please?"

Harvey was sure Darren would shake his head and walk away. He kept remembering Darren's face covered in purple splotches. But to Harvey's surprise, Darren took off his jacket. He was wearing his goalkeeper's shirt underneath.

"I'll need my gloves," he told Rita. "You get back in attack, where you belong."

The Team all cheered as Darren took his place in goal, and Harvey began to feel excited. The Team were back! And if they played their best, they were good enough to win …

Harvey kicked off and The Team kept the ball, passing it around.

Slowly, they edged towards the Diamonds' goal.

Soon Rita was in a position to shoot. She drew back her foot, then smiled and passed to Matt instead. "Would you like to take this shot, my good sir?" she asked politely.

"Why thank you, madam." Matt took a swipe at the ball, and it skidded towards the corner flag.

"Useless," said Rita, shaking her head. "Oh no — sorry, I meant to say: excellent try, Matt!"

Steffi laughed. So did Matt. But Harvey was annoyed. They'd had a chance, and they'd wasted it.

Harvey managed to intercept the ball and start another attack. He passed to Matt.

"Ladies first," said Matt. He passed it straight to Steffi.

"Thanks," said Steffi lightly. "But I think Harvey should have it. He *is* our captain, after all."

"What are you doing?" complained Harvey. Diamonds players were swarming around him. He managed to flick the ball over their heads to Rita, who had a clear path ahead.

But Rita passed it straight back to him, even though he was still surrounded.

"Why don't you do one of your brilliant runs?" Rita encouraged him. "You know, where you take on the whole defence and score."

Harvey twisted and turned his way through the Diamonds. To his surprise, he still had the ball at his feet. He looked around for someone to pass to, but they were all too busy laughing. Harvey couldn't believe it. He was glad that they weren't arguing anymore, but now they were joking around so much they weren't taking the game seriously!

Harvey put on some speed to outrun a Diamonds midfielder. He was heading towards the Diamonds' goal, but there were at least five Diamonds players in his way. There was nowhere to go except straight at them.

Harvey slowed down, turning left, right, pushing the ball through defenders' legs until he stumbled and started to fall. He felt a sudden anger at The Team. Why couldn't they just play like they used to? If they'd helped him, instead of standing around laughing, they might have had a goal.

As Harvey tumbled to the ground, he stretched and irritably kicked the ball away. The Diamonds goalie cried out in dismay as the ball shot into his goal.

The Team went wild, skidding through the mud to Harvey.

"When we enjoy ourselves, we're the best!" declared Steffi.

"But we've got to play *properly*," Harvey urged them. "If we do that, we can have fun *and* win!"

The Diamonds kicked off, attacking fiercely, and The Team settled down in defence. At half-time the score was still one–one.

Harvey was glowing. "If the score stays like this, we'll win the league!" he said. "And ..."

"No," said Steffi. "If we win, we win. But if we start thinking about it, we'll only get nervous and start arguing again."

"Forget about winning," said Matt.

But Harvey couldn't forget about it.

The second half started like the first had ended, with the Diamonds attacking furiously. The Team were worn out from defending, and had hardly any energy left to attack. But they held on, and at last Harvey saw the ref check his watch.

Harvey almost cheered. The Team were going to draw the game and win the league!

Matt cleared the ball from defence and Harvey collected it. He turned to attack, dodged a defender, then shouted in frustration when the defender tackled him.

"Cool it," Rita said as she ran back to defend again. "Remember, be happy!"

Harvey was too nervous to be happy. The Team only had to keep the Diamonds from scoring for another few minutes!

The Diamonds defender booted the ball high and long over everyone's heads. Darren held up his arms to catch it after it bounced.

But the ball didn't bounce.

It landed with a slap in the swampy goal area, skidded through Darren's legs, and trickled into the goal.

It was the worst goalkeeping mistake Harvey had ever seen. Without thinking, he raced towards Darren. He wasn't going to wait for The Team to start shouting — this time, he was going to do it himself!

Chapter 7

Harvey tore down the field. Darren had lost them everything. They'd have been better off without him.

But as he reached the goal area, Harvey started to slip. He fell onto his back with a SPLAT! and shot across the watery mud, which sloshed up the legs of his shorts and inside his shirt but didn't slow him down. Just like the ball had a minute before, Harvey skidded straight through Darren's legs.

When he stood up, he had to spit out a mouthful of mud. He used his little fingers to clear mud from his ears — and then he heard The Team roaring with laughter.

"I'm not complaining," said Steffi, who was standing over Darren shaking her head. "But that was RUBBISH!" She started clucking so hard she was barely able to breathe.

"It wasn't a very good save, was it?" said Darren, shaking his head. "I couldn't even save Harvey!"

Harvey started to giggle. He felt mud trickling down his ribs, and squeezing its way out in lumps from his shorts, and he laughed. He had to keep stopping to spit out more mud, but thinking about how he'd skidded through Darren's legs made him start laughing all over again. It felt like all his anger was rising harmlessly into the sky like the rainbow-coloured smoke from Professor Gertie's tower, leaving him warm and happy.

"It's not your fault," he said to Darren. "It must be like goalkeeping on an ice rink."

"It's worse," said Darren. "But I'm sorry we're going to lose."

"Don't worry," said Harvey. "The Team are cured, and that's all that matters."

The ref blew his whistle, checked his watch again, and The Team kicked off. The Diamonds stayed back in defence.

"One minute to go!" yelled Professor Gertie and Mark 1 together through the Shouting Mask.

Harvey watched them jumping up and down, and was doubly happy that they were enjoying themselves so much. The Team didn't have to win. All they had to do was play together and be happy.

Rita had the ball. There were eleven Diamonds players between her and the Diamond's goal.

"Your turn to score," said Harvey with a friendly smile.

Rita laughed. Her legs always turned to jelly when she got near the goal. Everyone knew that. But now that there was no pressure, she might as well have some fun.

She approached the defenders slowly, as if she was trying to work out a way through the maze of legs.

"Yes!" Harvey shouted as Rita passed one defender, then he clapped as she skipped past two more.

CRUNCH! Harvey winced, but Rita was still on her feet, and she was inside the Diamonds' goal area. Suddenly, Harvey felt a jolt of excitement. There was a space opening up in front of the goal. If Rita bore left, she'd have a clear shot!

Harvey tried not to think about it. If she scored, she scored. He watched her burst through two defenders into the space he had seen. She only had the goalie to beat. She lined up the shot and —

"Ow!" Rita yelled in pain as a defender crashed into her from behind, sending her crashing into the mud.

Harvey had no idea why The Team were cheering as they helped her to her feet. Then he heard the ref blow his whistle, and turned to see him pointing to the penalty spot.

Harvey felt a hundred butterflies flap inside his stomach. They had a penalty!

"Harvey takes it!" said Rita, grinning as she limped back to them.

Harvey's stomach lurched. His face felt hot and cold, and he kept touching it to see if he could feel any purple splotches. "It's not my penalty!" he pleaded.

"You take it, Rita," said Steffi. "It's yours."

Rita went pale. "No. I can't. You take it."

Steffi folded her arms tightly. "Uh-uh. Matt can take it."

"No way!" said Matt.

The ref looked at his watch.

"Someone take the penalty!" Harvey said desperately. "The ref might take it away!"

Everyone was frowning and looking angry. Was this the end of The Team after all, arguing over who would take the most important penalty they'd ever had? Harvey couldn't believe it, but he knew he didn't have the nerve to take it — and neither did anyone else.

Darren trotted up. "What's the problem?" he said. "If no one else wants to take it, I will."

The Team gasped. "What about the pressure?" said Harvey. "You'll get purple splotches!"

"I get those from *bad* pressure," said Darren. "Like when people are blaming me all the time. Taking this penalty is *good* pressure. If I score, we win and I'm a hero. If I miss, no one can complain because no one else wants to take it. Right?"

The Team all nodded.

Darren placed the ball on the penalty spot. He waited for the ref to blow his whistle, then he took two steps up to the ball and blasted it.

"**Goal!**" screamed Professor Gertie and Mark 1.

But the Diamonds goalkeeper pushed the ball to the side, where it hit the goalpost, and rebounded back out — straight to Darren.

This time, Darren calmly fired the ball straight into the centre of the goal.

The Team were stunned to silence.

"No problem," said Darren as the final whistle was blown. "Soccer Camp, here we come!

SOCCER CAMP

Chapter 1

"We're here!" shouted Harvey.

The Team cheered as their bus turned off the main road. It swung past a white building with a sign saying "Soccer Camp" above its wide glass doors, and stopped in a car park surrounded by trees.

Rita joined Harvey at the window as he watched people in yellow baseball caps setting up a small stage on a field. "There are *three* pitches!" he told her excitedly.

"Watch out!" they both cried as they were crushed against the window by Professor Gertie and Mark 1.

"Make room!" said Professor Gertie. "We want to see too!" Professor Gertie was Harvey's inventor neighbour — and The Team's greatest fan. She squeezed between Rita and Harvey.

"I can't believe we're actually at Soccer Camp," Harvey said. "This is where the *real* players come to train."

"You're here because you won the league," said Professor Gertie proudly.

Mark 1 stood on the seat to peer over them. He was The Team's trainer, and Professor Gertie's best-ever invention: a Football Machine.

Mark 1 spoke in his strange mechanical voice. "Thanks, Harvv."

Harvey looked at him — and jumped. "What are you wearing?!"

Professor Gertie lowered her voice as Steffi and Matt jostled past, fighting to be first off the bus. "It's a disguise," she explained.

Rita laughed. "He just looks like a robot with a false nose, moustache and glasses!"

"No one will notice," said Professor Gertie, trying to sound confident.

"But why does he need to wear it?" asked Harvey.

"Well …" Professor Gertie looked flustered. "You're always telling me robots aren't allowed to play on The Team."

"The referees don't like them," Harvey agreed.

"But Mark 1 deserves to be here, doesn't he?" Professor Gertie went on.

"Of course he does," said Rita. "We'd never won a single game until Mark 1 began coaching us."

"Well then," said Professor Gertie, as if that explained everything.

"I still don't understand," said Rita.

Professor Gertie said awkwardly, "The teams that come to Soccer Camp have to bring two Responsible Adults with them. Since Mark 1 can't be on The Team, he has to be a grown-up, like me."

Harvey looked at Rita, and knew what she was thinking. Even with a moustache, Mark 1 didn't look anything like a Responsible Adult. His head was made from an upturned rubbish bin and, still visible behind the false glasses, his eyes were red lights, like the scanners at a supermarket checkout.

Professor Gertie looked around. "Where has everybody gone?" she said. "They should have waited for the Responsible Adults to lead them off the bus!"

Harvey and Rita followed Professor Gertie and Mark 1 as they trotted across the car park, trying to catch up with the rest of The Team.

Professor Gertie kept looking around uneasily, and as they passed along the side of the white building, where tables and chairs were being set up, she tried to shield Mark 1 with her lab coat.

"This is silly!" laughed Rita. "Who cares if we brought a robot anyway?"

Professor Gertie didn't say anything.

"Would we be in trouble?" said Harvey.

Professor Gertie pretended not to hear.

"You have to tell us!" said Rita.

Professor Gertie glanced over each shoulder, then reached into her pocket and took out an envelope. "I don't think they'd actually *do* it," she said.

"Do WHAT?" shouted Harvey and Rita together.

"Here, you read it." Professor Gertie handed Harvey a letter. He read out loud,

"Dear Team,

Congratulations! You have won a place at Soccer Camp, the training centre for professional players.

Every year, three of the best junior teams from around the country are invited to compete for the Soccer Camp Cup.

All teams MUST be accompanied by TWO Responsible Adults.

Any team that breaks the rules will be sent home immediately."

Harvey felt his guts tying themselves up in nervous knots. Winning this trip to Soccer Camp was the best thing that had ever happened to him — losing the chance to play even a single game would be the worst.

"They wouldn't send us home," said Rita. "They couldn't!"

"They could," said Harvey gloomily. "And as soon as they realise Mark 1 isn't a Responsible Adult, they will."

Chapter 2

"Nonsense!" said Professor Gertie. "We won't be sent anywhere as long as we don't draw attention to ourselves. Now hurry up — we're late."

Harvey shoved the letter in his pocket as he and Rita jogged up to join the rest of The Team, who were sitting on the field in front of a man wearing a yellow baseball cap with "Coach" written on the front. The coach had flabby cheeks and tight lips that looked like they spent most of their time blowing a whistle.

Two other teams were grouped on the ground as well, but Harvey didn't have time to check them out properly because the coach was wagging a finger at him and Rita.

"You're late!" he barked. "And where are your adults?"

Professor Gertie blustered up, holding Mark 1 behind her with one arm. The robot was jumping up and down in his built-in Bouncing Boots, craning to see over her head.

"It's lucky we haven't unpacked our bags yet," Harvey whispered to Rita, "because we're going straight back on the bus!"

The coach frowned. "Are you The Team's adults?" he asked Professor Gertie and Mark 1.

"Yep, Sssir!" declared Mark 1 at the top of an extra-high bounce.

The coach rubbed his eyes.

"Are you sure you're old enough?"

"Yep, Sssir!" said Mark 1, his false nose, moustache and glasses wobbling dangerously.

"We're definitely adults!" broke in Professor Gertie quickly. "We're *very* responsible, too. We're not in disguise, or anything!"

Harvey covered his face with his hands, feeling his heart thump in his chest. This was it. They were about to be sent home. But to his surprise, the coach clapped his hands once and said, "Okay, teams — welcome to Soccer Camp!"

And everybody around Harvey and Rita cheered.

Harvey listened closely while the coach explained what they would be doing during their two days at Soccer Camp. The teams would play each other for the Camp Cup. And there would be a strategy session. Harvey couldn't wait for that. All the best teams had strategies. They were essential.

"The first game after lunch will be The Team against the Termites," announced the coach before leading them back to the main building, where cardboard sandwich boxes were being laid out on tables by the same yellow-capped people Harvey had seen setting up the stage.

The first team to line up were small and wiry, and each player wore a T-shirt with "The Mighty Termites" written on the back.

"They look more like the *tiny* Termites to me!" Steffi scoffed, and The Team laughed. Harvey had already noticed something about the Termites, though. They had formed a neat queue, and as each player grabbed a box, they turned and walked back to the field in an orderly line.

"They're well-organised," he told Rita, who nodded.

Professor Gertie pushed in front of Harvey, chose a box and bustled away, leaving Mark 1 behind. "I'm just going to get the bags off the bus!" she called.

The Team carried their lunch past the Termites and onto the empty pitch. Harvey made sure Mark 1 was hidden in the middle of the group when they sat down to eat.

"Look!" Darren pointed as the third team trekked past them to the furthest pitch.

"They're huge!"

"They look like a herd of rhinos," said Rita.

"You don't get herds of rhinos," said Steffi. "Anyway, they're called the Buffalos."

"Same thing," said Rita. "We're still going to get trampled."

"No way," said Matt confidently. "They might look beefy, but The Team wouldn't be here if we weren't a match for them."

"We should make the most of it," Harvey said, watching Mark 1, who had pushed his false nose, moustache and glasses up onto his forehead to keep the sun out of his eyes. "We might not be here for very long." He took the Soccer Camp letter from his pocket and handed it around.

"Is Mark 1 supposed to be our Responsible Adult?" said Steffi after she'd read the letter, shaking her head in disbelief.

Harvey nodded.

"But when they find out, we'll be sent home!" Steffi said.

Rita tried to cheer everyone up. "We'll be okay. The coach was completely fooled by Mark 1's disguise. What could go wro—?"

Even before she'd finished speaking, a blast of cold water hit her square in the face, almost knocking her backwards.

The Team sprang up, ducking and dodging as more spray hit them.

"Where's it coming from?" yelled Harvey.

"Everywhere!" shouted Darren.

"This way!" said Harvey, making a dash for the sideline but skidding on the slippery grass. The rest of The Team tripped over him, making one big, soggy heap.

The water stopped as suddenly as it had started.

Harvey felt Mark 1's metal head crushing his ribs. Wriggling out of the crush, he heard a noise and looked up.

The Buffalos and Termites were bellowing and squealing as if they'd just seen the funniest thing in the world.

"We were supposed to be keeping a low profile!" Harvey said despairingly.

"At least it can't get any worse," muttered Rita.

Click!

"It just has," said Harvey. Someone had taken their picture.

Chapter 3

Professor Gertie came rushing up. "You're soaked! What happened?" she shrieked.

"The sprinklers must be playing up again," said the coach, who was right behind her. "But don't worry, everyone has to change into their kit for the photo shoot."

"Photo shoot?" said Steffi, her eyes widening.

"You've got five minutes," said the coach, checking his watch.

Professor Gertie led the way to two wooden huts tucked among the trees. "Boys are to the right, girls to the left," she said. "I've already put your bags inside."

She took the girls away and Harvey led Mark 1 and the boys into their hut, where they found two rows of bunkbeds. Sitting tidily on those nearest the door were small bags with a picture of a termite on the front.

"The Mites must have got here first," Matt complained.

Further in, there was a jumble of enormous backpacks.

"The Beefs," commented Matt as he stepped over them.

The Team's bags were leaning against the bunks at the back of the room.

Professor Gertie came in, holding a large bundle in her arms. "My new invention!" she declared.

Harvey handed out the shiny red shirts, white shorts, and red socks.

"Nice bit of cloth!" said Darren, who was holding up his brand-new silver-edged goalkeeper's jersey.

"My Supercloth is indestructible!" said Professor Gertie. "It never loses its shine, never tears, and never wears out."

Harvey helped Mark 1 out of his wet clothes, then he slipped his own new shirt over his head. It smelled like a fresh bar of soap.

"Supercloth is coated with Self-Cleaning Sudsoap," Professor Gertie continued. "Mud and stains fall off while you wear it. I'll never have to wash filthy sportswear again!"

She hurried back to the girls' hut just as the Termites and Buffalos barged in, changed at top speed, and tramped out again.

The Team were still struggling with their shorts. Then Professor Gertie called from the door in a high, embarrassed voice. "Er … it seems there may be a problem with the Easy-Fix Shorts. I'll tie them up for you on your way out."

Harvey was searching under the beds. "I can't find my bag," he told Darren as the rest of The Team stamped out behind Mark 1.

"Hurry, boys!" called Professor Gertie.

"Just put your kit on," said Darren. "We can find your bag later."

"I can't," said Harvey.

"Why not?" said Darren.

"I just *can't*."

"Why?" said Darren.

"Because," Harvey said, his voice rising, "I haven't got any dry underpants!"

He sat down on a bed. "You go," he said. "I'll wait here."

"But — the photo shoot," said Darren.

Suddenly Professor Gertie's hand appeared in the doorway. Dangling from her fingers were the shiny red Fireproof Underpants Harvey had worn with the Smoke Machine, one of Professor Gertie's first inventions for The Team.

"Harvey, please stop shouting and put these on," she said urgently. "Darren, you come with me. I can't be late again — I'm a Responsible Adult!"

Harvey changed as fast as he could. But when he pulled on his shorts they were baggy and loose, and the ties were at the back, out of his reach. Holding them up with one hand, he raced back to the field.

The teams were grouped onto the small stage Harvey had seen from the bus. The Buffalos were squashed together on the left, the Termites were lined up neatly in the middle, and The Team were gathered on the right.

Harvey ran up just in time to hear the photographer introducing herself. He quickly squeezed into a space right at the front of The Team.

"I'm Karen Cascarino," the woman said. "But you can call me KC. I've been sent from *Soccer Stars* magazine, and —"

Steffi screamed with delight. Harvey knew why — *Soccer Stars* was the top football magazine in the country.

"I'd like to begin with a group shot of all the teams," continued KC. "Can the, er, Buffalos move back a bit so I can fit you in?"

The Buffalos shuffled backwards.

"The Termites can come closer, and," said KC, pointing at Steffi, "can you please return to your team?"

Steffi, no longer in position, was standing at the front of the stage with a dazzling smile on her face. "My name is Stefanie Bush," she said. "That's Stefanie with an 'f'."

"Thank you, Miss Bush," said KC, waiting patiently.

But Steffi didn't move, or stop smiling.

"What's up with Steffi?" Harvey whispered to Matt, but Matt just shook his head.

"Miss Bush!" said KC irritably as she crouched down to take the picture.

"Okay, okay," said Steffi sulkily. She pushed her way back to her place, nearly jostling Harvey off the stage. "Move over!" she hissed.

"I can't!" said Harvey. "There's no room."

Steffi tried to shove him out of the way with her elbow, and knocked his hand off his shorts, which fell all the way down to his ankles.

Click! Click! Click!

"Superb!" laughed KC. Harvey saw her camera zoom in on his underpants.

"They're not mine!" he said desperately as everyone turned to see.

The Termites squealed.

"They're Professor Gertie's fireproof ones!" Harvey explained.

The Buffalos bellowed.

Harvey tried to make them understand. "I only wear them when I'm going to make smoke!"

The sound of the camera clicking was drowned out by bellowing and squealing. Harvey wondered which would come out brightest in *Soccer Stars* magazine — his shiny underpants, or his glowing face.

Chapter 4

"You're really funny," said KC, holding Harvey's arm as he tried to get away after the photo shoot. "What's your name?"

"Harvey Bighead Boots!" yelled Steffi.

"It's not," said Harvey. "It's just Harvey Boots."

KC scribbled in her notebook. "Okay, Just Harvey Boots, have you always wanted to be a comedian?"

"No, he hasn't!" hollered Steffi. "But he wants to steal the limelight from everyone else!"

"I wasn't trying to be funny," said Harvey. "I lost my bag so I didn't have any dry, er, things. Professor Gertie must have brought her Inventing Box with her. She gave me the, er, whatsits that I wear with the Smoke Machine."

"That's very interesting," said KC. "Who's

Professor Gertie? What else has she invented?"

"I have to go!" said Harvey, and he bolted away, holding onto his shorts tightly. The last thing he wanted to do was talk about Professor Gertie's inventions. Next thing, KC would find out about Mark 1.

Harvey found Darren, Matt and Rita waiting for him outside the huts.

"Hard luck, Harvey," said Darren.

"Rubbish," said Steffi, striding up to them. "Harvey's got KC begging for an interview. Talk about showing off!"

"What are you on about?" said Rita.

"This is a chance for *all* of us to be in *Soccer Stars*," said Steffi. "Not just Harvey."

"Why do you want to be in *Soccer Stars* so much?" said Darren.

Steffi rolled her eyes. "So I'd be famous, of course!"

"Famous for what?" Matt butted in. "You haven't done anything."

"Just *famous*!" said Steffi impatiently.

"Famous for being famous?" Matt laughed.

"Yes!" said Steffi. "Everybody wants to be famous."

The others looked at each other, and shrugged.

"Harvey does," she said. "That's why he was joking around for KC. This proves it." She picked up Harvey's bag, which was lying by the side of the huts as if someone had dropped it there.

"You probably hid it here yourself," Steffi said, throwing it to Harvey. "I bet you had those Fireproof Bloomers ready, too."

"I didn't!" Harvey protested. But Steffi turned her back on him and stalked off.

While Harvey checked his bag to make sure he had a spare pair of underpants, Darren admitted, "I wouldn't mind being famous for being a great goalie. Like, if I saved every shot for a year."

"That's being famous for doing something," said Rita. "Not just for being a pretty face."

Matt looked surprised. "Can you be famous for that? Cool!" He smiled the way Steffi did when KC was there.

"Sshh!" Professor Gertie tiptoed from the girls' hut. "Fame is a dangerous thing. If that woman finds out about Mark 1, she won't stop pestering until she's got the whole story! We'll be *exposed*!"

"Why would she be interested in Mark 1?" said Matt.

Professor Gertie glared at him. "Mark 1 is one of the most sophisticated robots ever made!" she said. "*And* he's a soccer genius. He could fill a magazine all by himself!"

"Where is he now?" asked Harvey.

"Making himself invisible," said Professor Gertie.

Harvey heard heavy feet clomp down the steps of the boys' hut, and turned around. Mark 1 looked the same as before, except for a yellow baseball cap that was stretched so tightly over his rubbish-bin head it looked like a swimming cap.

The sound of Matt's laughter was drowned out by a long, piercing whistle.

"The game must be starting!" said Professor Gertie. "Harvey, go change your pants!"

Harvey ran inside to get changed. When he came out, he was relieved to see Professor Gertie waiting to tie his shorts.

"I do hope Mark 1 keeps his head down," she said worriedly. "But I think he'll blend in now, don't you?"

As they arrived on the field, Harvey saw that Mark 1 definitely did not blend in. Even though he was standing with The Team all around him, the bright yellow cap made him stand out as if a spotlight was shining on his head. KC was already pushing past people to get to him.

"Hello!" Harvey heard her say. "You came with Harvey Boots, didn't you? What can you tell me about him? Has he got a girlfriend? And tell me about this Professor Gertie …"

Harvey listened anxiously, but the coach drowned out Mark 1's replies. "We play thirty minutes each half, with ten minutes in between," he said.

Harvey heard KC say, "… and what else has she invented to help The Team? Apart from the Fireproof Underp —"

Professor Gertie nudged Harvey. "We have to stop her!" she said, her eyes bulging. The coach started speaking again before Harvey could respond.

"We'll be ready to start as soon as an assistant referee arrives," said the coach, looking around. "Is there anyone here with a yellow cap? All yellow-capped camp workers are fully trained referees. Aha! There's one!" The coach beckoned to Mark 1. "Don't just stand there!"

Harvey heard Professor Gertie groan as the coach put an orange flag into Mark 1's hand. "Oh no!" she said. "I found the cap in one of the huts! It's my fault!"

"The Team can kick off," said the coach as the players jogged onto the field.

Harvey joined Rita at the centre spot and watched KC, who was standing on the sideline with Soccer Camp's newest line referee. While KC lifted what looked like a small telescope

from her handbag, Mark 1 pressed his chest. Harvey knew there was a button under the robot's shirt, and that pressing it once began a warm-up routine.

"I've got a *very* bad feeling about this," Harvey said as the Football Machine stretched and whirred, and KC began taking pictures. How many seconds would it be before Mark 1 was found out? He started counting: one, two, three … Then he yelped when the coach blew a whistle close to his ear.

"Kick off, Harvey!" called Matt from defence. "Let's see how many goals we can score before the break!"

Harvey tapped the ball to Rita as energy flooded through him, like it always did at the start of a game. His worries about Mark 1 floated to the back of his mind. Now was his chance to find out how good the Termites really were …

He didn't get another kick of the ball until ten long minutes later.

Chapter 5

They were like ants, Harvey decided. It didn't matter how small they were, because they were everywhere.

Whenever The Team got the ball, three or four Termites players swarmed in to retrieve it. Harvey was hoping they would soon run out of breath, but they showed no signs of tiring.

"This is embarrassing!" said Matt.

For the third time in a row, he'd lost the ball to a Termites forward right in front of Darren's goal. Darren came running out, trying for yet another save, but there was nothing he could do as a Termites attacker chipped the ball neatly towards the open net.

Harvey glimpsed someone in a red shirt streaking across to intercept. At first, the sun shining yellow on the player's head gave Harvey the dreadful feeling that it was Mark 1 … but then he recognized Steffi's long blonde hair sailing out behind her.

With a flying kick, Steffi launched the ball

upfield to Harvey, who immediately lost it to two Termites midfielders.

"Nice save!" Matt called to Steffi.

"Fantastic, more like!" said Darren.

Steffi didn't reply. Harvey saw that she was ignoring the game completely as she smiled towards KC, who was holding her camera ready.

Click!

The Termites launched a ferocious assault and Harvey ran back to help The Team defend.

"I hope she gets me in some action shots," Steffi told him as he passed her. "Wait a minute, aren't you supposed to be in attack?"

"Yes!" said Harvey sharply. "But you're too busy posing to defend!"

It was useless. Harvey was too far behind the Termites forwards, who quickly hustled the ball through The Team's defence. Again, Darren didn't stand a chance, and this time there was nobody to stop the ball sailing into the goal.

"One–nil to the Mites," huffed Matt. "Thanks to our most *famous* defender!"

"We're lucky it isn't more," said Darren as The Team collapsed in the goal area at half-time. "They're running rings around us."

"They seem to read each other's minds," complained Rita.

"They work together," said Harvey simply. "They're a brilliant team."

For the rest of the break they watched Professor Gertie chasing after Mark 1, who was keeping one step ahead of her as he juggled his flag and cap. KC was snapping pictures of the pair of them.

"Stop it!" they heard Professor Gertie shouting at Mark 1. "You're supposed to be incognito!"

"Poor Mark 1," said Rita. "He only wants to have some fun."

Harvey saw that the coach was ready to start. "Let's give it our best," he said to The Team encouragingly. "We haven't had a shot yet!"

Midway through the second half, with The Team still battling in defence, Rita managed to scoop the ball to Harvey's feet. He turned quickly and dodged two Termites midfielders. There was no one to pass to, so he coasted down the right side of the pitch, giving The Team time to get forward. The Termites' defence crowded him towards their corner flag, and to his frustration Harvey found himself blocked in.

Suddenly he caught sight of a wave of red shirts breaking into the penalty area. The Team was on the attack! He fired the ball towards them, then watched glumly as it passed uselessly over their heads and curled towards the edge of the goal area. It looked to Harvey like it was going to land on Matt, who was the last to arrive.

"Look out, Matt!" he called.

Matt ducked, but he was too late. The ball slammed against the side of his head — and bounced straight into the top corner of the net!

"GOAL!" cried Professor Gertie.

Matt stumbled, rolled over twice and stood back up, looking dazed as Harvey raced across to congratulate him.

Click! Click! Click!

"Spectacular!" exclaimed KC.

Matt grinned.

"Oh, you've got a *perfect* smile! But you're not just a pretty face, are you?"

Click! Click! Click!

Harvey saw that Matt was still grinning as he returned to The Team's defence.

The Termites kicked off, lost the ball to Harvey, and retreated as The Team tried for another goal.

"What's your name?" called KC.

"Who, me?" said Matt, who was hovering by the halfway line. "I'm Matt."

"Matt what?"

He strolled over to the sideline. "Matt —"

"Stay in position!" hollered Harvey as he

was tackled and the Termites counterattacked, bursting through the gap Matt had left in defence. Matt scrambled desperately for the ball, but the Termites scurried past him and Darren for an easy goal.

Matt groaned.

Click!

"That's more like you," snapped Steffi. "*Soccer Stars* has a page at the back for pictures like that, though usually they only show people's ugly pets!"

From then on The Team had trouble keeping the Termites from scoring again, and Harvey was the lone striker as Rita bolstered the defence. On the few occasions he got the ball he had nobody to pass to, and the Termites took it from him easily.

Harvey saw the coach put his whistle to his mouth and called, "Last chance — everybody forward!" He saw Mark 1 sprint along the sideline, his flag tucked under one arm, making a noise like a rocket taking off.

Matt came tearing up the field, calling for the ball and waving his arms like a windmill. The rest of The Team were behind him, streaming towards the Termites' goal. They all knew that if they didn't score, they'd lose. Defending was pointless now.

Steffi hassled the ball from a Termites defender, and sent it swerving into the goal area. Harvey quickened his pace ... But before he could reach the ball, another red-shirted player thundered in a diving header.

Harvey could hear the clicking of KC's camera even over the shriek of the final whistle, and all his hope turned to dismay as The Team's Responsible Adult cartwheeled down the pitch to celebrate his stupendous goal.

Chapter 6

The coach held up a red card and spluttered, "Goal not allowed — game over!" as Professor Gertie marched Mark 1 away. KC rushed after them, trailed by Steffi.

"Did you get my save off the line?" Harvey heard Steffi say.

As Professor Gertie and Mark 1 disappeared behind the trees, KC stopped and turned towards Steffi.

"Looks like she's getting her interview," Rita observed, adding hopefully, "Maybe she'll take KC's mind off Mark 1."

Harvey didn't reply. He was still standing in the goal mouth, replaying the last move of the game in his mind. The ball coming across from Steffi, his clear opportunity … he would probably have scored, he decided. If he had, The Team wouldn't have lost.

The coach was standing nearby, fuming

and looking like he wanted to blow his whistle at somebody. "That was no assistant referee!" Harvey heard him mutter.

"Let's go," Rita advised Harvey. As they followed the other teams back to the main building, she said, "I don't think we can fool the coach much longer. What are we going to do?"

Harvey felt depressed. "I just don't know," he said, sighing.

"This way," said Darren, holding a door open for them. "We get dinner inside. There's a cafeteria and everything."

They took trays from a kitchen hatch and looked for spaces to sit at one of the three long tables. Harvey spotted Professor Gertie at the furthest table, huddled behind the leaves of a palm tree growing from a pot.

"Sorreee, Harvv," said Mark 1 from underneath the table when Harvey, Rita and Darren sat down. Harvey was pleased to find Mark 1 was no longer wearing the yellow

baseball cap, but he hated to see the robot looking so miserable behind his false glasses.

"That's okay," Harvey said. "And it *was* a good goal." He smiled, and Mark 1's eyes flickered happily.

Professor Gertie leaned across to Harvey. "I don't think anyone noticed he isn't actually a Responsible Adult. But that woman with the camera is definitely getting suspicious — look, there she is!"

Professor Gertie plunged under the table as KC came in, closely followed by Steffi. "I don't know what to do!" Harvey heard Professor Gertie whining as she and Mark 1 crawled out through a side exit.

"Professor Gertie!" KC sailed towards their table, then stopped. "Oh, I thought I'd find Professor Gertie here," she said, turning to look meaningfully at Steffi, whose face had turned as red as the Fireproof Underpants. As KC walked away, Steffi kept at her heel.

"Did you see that?" Rita said urgently. "You don't think Steffi would have *told* KC about Professor Gertie and Mark 1?"

"She'd better not have," said Harvey grimly, turning to his plate and playing with his food. He was worried about Mark 1, but he couldn't think of anything to do. Then the Buffalos sat down noisily at the next table, and Harvey started thinking about The Team's other big

problem: how were they going to beat the giant-sized Beefs?

Harvey lined up his meatballs. They were the Buffalos. Facing them, he made The Team out of peas and oddly shaped bits of carrot, with a mashed brussel sprout in goal. For the rest of dinnertime, he pushed the players around on his plate. The meatballs were always too big. There was no way around them.

Darren nudged his shoulder. "We have to go," he said. They trailed behind the other teams into a large gym, where they all sat on the floor in front of a television.

"A movie!" said Matt, who then groaned loudly when the words "Soccer Strategy" appeared on the screen.

The video showed bits from famous World Cup games. Harvey had seen some of them before. Every now and then the coach would stop the tape and say things like, "Play to your strengths. Winning teams do what they're good at."

The room was hot, and everyone began to doze, even Harvey. Watching wasn't giving him any ideas, and he was relieved when the teams were at last led back to their huts.

Harvey lay down on his bed and closed his eyes. As the others began to snore all around him, he tried to relax. If KC finds out about Mark 1, he said to himself, at least we won't have to play the Buffalos. We'll be going home instead!

Harvey was soon dreaming that the *Soccer Stars* reporter was following him everywhere, longing to know the secret of Mark 1. She was spoiling everything he did by bugging him with questions. Harvey tugged his blankets over his head, and kept undercover ...

Chapter 7

Harvey felt his covers being yanked away and tried to hold on. "No pictures!" he screeched, before realising it wasn't KC.

"It's me," said Darren as everyone around them laughed. "The coach just told us that breakfast is ready, and there'll be nothing left if we don't get a move on."

Harvey pulled on his kit, trying to shake off his dreams of being hounded by KC, but he couldn't help checking all the windows to make sure she wasn't spying on him. Then, as he left the hut, he spotted her running along the path to the main building. She was heading towards Professor Gertie and Mark 1, who appeared to have no idea they were being followed.

Harvey pelted after them, ignoring calls from Darren. Professor Gertie and Mark 1 rounded the corner of the building, and KC

dashed around after them. Harvey reached the turn seconds later, skidded around, and found — nobody.

He ran to the big glass doors and pushed them open. There was just an empty office. He checked the cafeteria, then the gym. There was no sign of Professor Gertie, Mark 1 *or* KC.

Darren arrived, with Rita close behind.

"What's the matter?" panted Rita. "Why did you take off like that?"

"KC followed Professor Gertie and Mark 1 here," said Harvey. "Now they've *all* disappeared."

"They must be hiding," said Darren. "They could be anywhere."

"What's going on?" demanded Steffi, marching up to them. "Are you talking about me?"

"No," said Rita. "Should we be?"

Steffi opened her mouth to say something, but no words came out.

"How come you're so cosy with KC all of a sudden?" Rita pressed her. "You didn't tell her about Mark 1, did you?"

Steffi's face turned pink.

"You did!" said Rita, aghast.

"I told her my life story," Steffi said defiantly. "And Mark 1 is part of it, that's all. *Soccer Stars* readers deserve the truth."

She turned on her heel and walked away, leaving her three team mates staring at her with shocked expressions.

Harvey felt numb. "That's it," he said. "We're done for."

"I saw KC with the coach during the video last night," said Darren. "They were whispering about something."

Harvey sighed as the smell of cooking wafted from the cafeteria. "We might as well eat something before the long bus ride home," he said gloomily.

While they ate, The Team joined them, talking enthusiastically about the games ahead. Harvey felt miserable. How could he tell his friends that their time at Soccer Camp was about to end?

Suddenly the coach came in and blew a short "pip!" on his whistle. Everyone fell silent. Harvey had a feeling like molten rock sinking in his stomach. But the coach held up a ball and said, "The Termites play the Buffalos in thirty minutes. After that we'll have a drink break, then the Buffalos play The Team."

Darren gave Harvey the thumbs up, grinning.

Harvey felt relief flood through him. "Why hasn't KC told him about Mark 1?" he asked Rita.

"Maybe she's keeping it to herself," said Rita. "For a *Soccer Stars* exclusive story."

Harvey imagined a picture of him and Mark 1 in the magazine, and to his surprise he felt his spirits rise. It wouldn't be so bad if he wasn't in there alone. He took a hungry bite of toast.

"Now that leaves us with one tiny little problem," said Rita.

"What's that?" said Harvey.

"If we want to win the Soccer Camp Cup," said Rita, "we have to beat the Buffalos. But don't worry — I have a feeling they're just big, slow and clumsy."

After breakfast, everyone headed to the field, and The Team sat down to watch as the Buffalos ploughed easily through the Termites.

"It's a massacre," said Rita after the Beefs had powered in their first goal. The Termites goalie had been knocked flat on his back, and there was an oversized boot mark on his chest.

Darren looked pale. "What are we going to do?" he asked Harvey.

Matt leaned across and said cheerily, "We're going to win, of course."

"And how are we supposed to do that?" said Rita.

"Harvey's got a plan," said Matt.

"Huh?" said Harvey. "What plan? I haven't got a plan!"

"You watched that video last night," said Matt. "You must have some ideas."

The Team all turned eagerly to Harvey.

"I think," he said weakly, "that we have to play to our strengths."

"And what are they?" said Steffi, coming over from where she'd been sitting on her own.

Harvey looked at his friends. What *were* their strengths? he wondered. They weren't all small and quick like the Termites, or big and strong like the Buffalos. Matt and Steffi were both good defenders, but they didn't play the same way. Steffi was fast and aggressive. Matt was slow and patient, only tackling when the time was right.

"We're all different," Harvey said at last, shrugging.

"Great," said Steffi disgustedly. "We haven't got *any* strengths. Remind me to tell KC when she gets here. We don't want her to make a mistake when she writes about us in *Soccer Stars*."

Rita looked angrily at Steffi, but before she could say anything there was a loud roar as the Buffalos blasted home their second goal, and The Team watched the rest of the game in a moody silence.

Every now and then Harvey stood up and looked around, but he didn't see Professor Gertie, Mark 1 or KC anywhere.

"The Termites didn't do too badly," said Rita when the coach blew the final whistle, and the Buffalos gave a victory bellow. "They only lost three-nil. We should be able to draw, at least."

"You're forgetting that we lost to the Termites," said Harvey. "The Buffalos are going to slaughter us."

"*And*," added Darren, "The Team are in last

place, because we're the only ones who haven't won yet."

Rita looked crestfallen as they grabbed drinks from trays brought by the Soccer Camp workers.

"Remember, everyone," urged Matt, who had unexpectedly stood up to address The Team, "we need to win by *three* goals. If you want my advice, keep the pressure on until we're winning at least four–nil."

"I think scoring a goal has gone to his head," said Darren after Matt sat down. "But at least one of us is happy."

"I think we should just try to be ourselves, and do our own thing," said Rita. "What's the worst that could happen?"

"We lose," said Darren and Harvey together.

Suddenly Rita said loudly, "Oh, big deal!" And when Harvey choked on his drink, spilling it on his shirt, both she and Darren laughed.

"Professor Gertie won't be happy cleaning that!" said Darren.

"It doesn't matter," Harvey said with a grin. "Supercloth cleans itself, doesn't it?"

He wiped the liquid from his shirt with his hand. It came off bubbly and pink. "This drink's weird," he said.

Just then, the coach called the teams over to start the last game of Soccer Camp, and Harvey sprang lightly to his feet. The time for worrying was over.

Chapter 8

The first five minutes of the game against the Buffalos were the hardest The Team had ever known. The Beefs began their attacks slowly, but soon sped up into a stampede. It was dangerous to get in their way.

"Oof!" breathed Harvey as he was knocked sideways and landed on his face.

He lay stunned for a few seconds before pushing himself painfully to his feet, looking downfield at The Team milling around in defence. They were just like the peas and carrots he had pushed around his plate the evening before: they didn't stand a chance. The meatballs were unstoppable.

A Buffalos striker shot, and Darren pushed the ball away for a corner. As The Team took their usual positions to defend, Harvey imagined mashing up his peas and carrots with a fork, changing them into something new and unrecognisable. Something unexpected.

"Swap!" he shouted suddenly. "Matt, Steffi — everyone in defence change positions!"

The Team stared at him, puzzled.

"Are you sure?" said Rita.

"Won't that be, er, confusing?" said Darren.

"Do it!" said Matt, who was shoving Steffi out of his way to take her spot on the goal line. "This is Harvey's PLAN!"

The Team's defence reluctantly swapped places with each other. Harvey thought that the Buffalos were looking more confused than The Team, and when the ball came in from the corner, Matt cleared it by darting courageously between two huge forwards.

"They weren't expecting my pretty face!" Matt declared proudly. "Great strategy, Harv!"

From then on the Team's defence changed positions for every Buffalos attack.

"I don't believe it," Rita told Harvey, shaking her head. "But I think you've found a way to stop them!"

The Team began to put pressure on the Buffalos' goal. Harvey made a run, and Rita tried a long cross, but it was useless. The Beefs' tall goalkeeper reached over Harvey's head and caught the ball.

"Crosses are no good," Harvey told The Team at half-time.

"Any ideas how to score?" asked Rita.

"None," admitted Harvey.

"Me neither," said Rita.

As the Team kicked off the second half, Harvey was relieved to see Professor Gertie and Mark 1 arrive. And to his surprise, KC was with them. In fact, the three of them seemed

quite friendly. What was going on?

"Go for it, Mr Boots!" KC called, pointing her camera at him.

Harvey, who was looking towards KC, had the ball taken from him. He turned back to the game as the Buffalos' charge was again halted by The Team's changing defence.

"If we could only score," Harvey said to Rita as she sprinted past to receive the ball, "I think we could win!"

Rita threaded the ball to Harvey and he ran at the Buffalos' defence, feeling like he was inside a pinball machine as he rebounded from one giant defender to the next.

Rita tried a run herself but she was squashed by two Buffalos players halfway towards their goal. The coach awarded a free kick, and she placed the ball carefully on the grass.

"Don't bother crossing!" Harvey reminded her, but it looked like that was exactly what Rita was planning.

Harvey tried to find space among the Buffalos defenders, but there was barely room to move. The keeper came right out of his goal and stood behind Harvey with his hands held up, ready to catch the ball.

"They know what you're going to do!" Harvey shouted, but it was too late. Rita was already stepping up to the ball, and she booted it long and high. It whizzed wide to the right of Harvey. He heard the Buffalos goalie gasp, saw Rita raise her arms, then spun around in time to watch the ball bounce into the Buffalos' unguarded goal.

"Yes!" Harvey whispered, his voice rising to a delighted cry. "Yes!"

"They weren't expecting a shot on goal!" said Darren as The Team lifted Rita off her feet.

"Nobody was!" said Harvey.

"Except me!" Rita corrected them. "I knew what I was going to do all along. Now put me down!"

For the rest of the match, the Buffalos were forced to defend their goal, and despite The Team's efforts the score stayed the same. The Team won one–nil.

"Well done," said the coach briskly as The Team congratulated each other. "You work together, but everyone is allowed to play to their own strengths. And," he added, goggling at Mark 1 as the robot twirled Rita above his head, "The Team are *full* of surprises."

KC appeared at Harvey's side with her notebook in her hand. "Harvey Boots," she said. "You haven't won the Camp Cup, but you *have* beaten the Buffalos. How do you feel at this moment?"

"Er, great!" said Harvey, and then, unable to help himself, he posed for the camera.

Click!

Chapter 9

KC arranged the teams in a centre circle, the coach hung medals around all the players' necks, and the Buffalos were presented with the Soccer Camp Cup.

"Each team won a game," Matt explained to Harvey, "but the Beefs scored the most goals."

Click!

KC wrote down the Buffalos' names. Then

she closed her notebook, held up her camera and said to Harvey, "Got any more jokes, Mr Boots? I've only got one shot left."

Harvey shook his head.

The *Soccer Stars* reporter pretended to sulk, then stood back to frame everyone. "Smile, champs!"

Harvey felt a familiar drumming of water on his skull as the sprinklers rained down on them, but he didn't move. Nobody did. They were all holding their smiles as they waited for KC to take their picture.

The camera suddenly jerked towards The Team, and Harvey automatically put his hands to his shorts. Luckily, though, this time they hadn't fallen down, and he looked about to see who else had done something embarrassing.

Harvey started to giggle.

The Team were giving off bubbles! White bubbles from their shorts, and pink bubbles from their shirts.

Professor Gertie had her mouth open wide. "Oh!" she said. "It's my Supercloth! It never needs washing so I never tested it with water!"

The Team were nearly hidden by a mountain of soapsuds, and when KC finally took her last shot of Soccer Camp— click! — Harvey Boots was laughing loudest of all.

One week later The Team were in Professor Gertie's inventing tower, their eyes fixed on a large envelope. Darren read the message scrawled along the bottom.

"Thanks for being real, fun Soccer Stars! Love, KC."

Professor Gertie tore it open and held up the magazine. On the front there was a picture of the coach blowing his whistle.

"So *that's* why he was whispering with KC during the video!" said Rita. "Is everyone obsessed by fame?"

"Come on, look inside!" Steffi reached forward, turned the page — and gasped when a large picture of Professor Gertie smiled out at them.

Rita read, "Inventor and Soccer Fan Professor Gertie Gallop tells Karen Cascarino about her Inventing Box of tricks."

Steffi snatched the magazine and began skimming through it. It was full of Professor Gertie and her inventions. At least half of the pages were about Mark 1.

"YEP SSSIR!" the robot whooped, punching the air.

Steffi turned furiously to Professor Gertie. "KC was supposed to put *me* in *Soccer Stars*, but it's all about *you*! I thought you said fame was dangerous!"

"I met KC on the way to breakfast that last morning," explained Professor Gertie, blushing as she took the magazine back and bent to read it. "She said you had already told her about me and Mark 1, and I just wanted to give her the full story. I suppose everyone wants a little bit of celebrity," she added with a guilty grin.

"I don't," said Harvey, who was nervously scanning the pages as Professor Gertie turned them. Any time now, he thought, I'll see my underpants.

He didn't have long to wait.

They were in the centre of the magazine, in full colour. There was even a dotted line around them, so they could be cut out.

Darren read, "Are these The Team's latest secret weapon?"

Harvey glanced up to where he expected to see his own embarrassed face — and he almost collapsed with laughter.

"Look who's famous!" cackled Matt.

"Well done!" said Darren. "You've really made it — Steffi!"

Where Harvey's face should have been, there was a shot of Steffi flashing her biggest, brightest smile.

"It does serve you right, Steffi," Rita said coolly. "That's what happens to people who'd do anything for fame."

Harvey thought Steffi would see the funny side eventually — that is, when she'd stopped screaming.

David Bedford was born in Devon, in the south-west of England in 1969.

David wasn't always a writer. First he was a football player. He played for two teams: Appleton FC and Sankey Rangers. Although these weren't the worst teams in the league, they never won anything!

After school, David went to university and became a scientist. His first job was in America, where he worked on discovering new antibiotics.

David has always loved to read and decided to start writing stories himself. After a while, he left his job as a scientist and began writing full time. His novels and picture books have been translated into many languages around the world.

David lives with his wife and two children in Norfolk, England.